DATE DUE			

A NOTE TO PARENTS

Reading Aloud with Your Child
Research shows that reading books aloud is the single most valuable support parents can provide in helping children learn to read.
- Be a ham! The more enthusiasm you display, the more your child will enjoy the book.
- Run your finger underneath the words as you read to signal that the print carries the story.
- Leave time for examining the illustrations more closely; encourage your child to find things in the pictures.
- Invite your youngster to join in whenever there's a repeated phrase in the text.
- Link up events in the book with similar events in your child's life.
- If your child asks a question, stop and answer it. The book can be a means to learning more about your child's thoughts.

Listening to Your Child Read Aloud
The support of your attention and praise is absolutely crucial to your child's continuing efforts to learn to read.
- If your child is learning to read and asks for a word, give it immediately so that the meaning of the story is not interrupted. DO NOT ask your child to sound out the word.
- On the other hand, if your child initiates the act of sounding out, don't intervene.
- If your child is reading along and makes what is called a miscue, listen for the sense of the miscue. If the word "road" is substituted for the word "street," for instance, no meaning is lost. Don't stop the reading for a correction.
- If the miscue makes no sense (for example, "horse" for "house"), ask your child to reread the sentence because you're not sure you understand what's just been read.
- Above all else, enjoy your child's growing command of print and make sure you give lots of praise. *You are your child's first teacher—and the most important one. Praise from you is critical for further risk-taking and learning.*

—Priscilla Lynch
Ph.D., New York University
Educational Consultant

For Fred Margulies,
who always says yes
—T.S.

For Bridget
and her great sense of style
—M.J.

Library of Congress Cataloging-in-Publication Data available.

ISBN 0-590-44186-8

Text copyright © 1993 by Teddy Slater.
Illustrations copyright © 1993 by Meredith Johnson.
All rights reserved. Published by Scholastic Inc.
CARTWHEEL BOOKS is a trademark of Scholastic Inc.
HELLO READER! is a registered trademark of Scholastic Inc.

12 11 10 9 8   5 6 7 8/9

Printed in the U.S.A.   23

First Scholastic printing, March 1993

N-O Spells NO!

by Teddy Slater
Illustrated by Meredith Johnson

Hello Reader!—Level 2

Cartwheel
·B·O·O·K·S·®

SCHOLASTIC INC.

New York   London   Toronto   Auckland   Sydney

Katie was such a stubborn child.
She drove her mother nearly wild.

Kate ate meatballs for breakfast

and pancakes at night.

Her clothes never matched.

Her room was a fright.

There was only one way
Kate would get into bed—

with her feet on the pillow,
her head on the spread.

When her mother said RED,
Kate was sure to say BLUE.

When her mother said ONE,
you can bet Kate said TWO.

When her mother said STOP,
Kate just had to say GO.

But her favorite words
were N-O spells NO!

Kate said N-O to liver
and broccoli, too,
stuck up her nose
and said N-O! P-U!

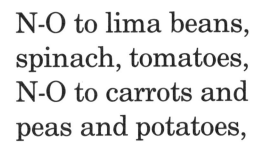

N-O to lima beans,
spinach, tomatoes,
N-O to carrots and
peas and potatoes,

NO to hot oatmeal
and cold cottage cheese,
N-O spells NO!—

not even "No, please."

There were more NO's for naptime

and at bathtime, too,

tooth brushing...

hair combing...
tying her shoe.
There were millions of things
Katie just wouldn't do!

She would not put her toys away.
She would not flush the potty.

She would not wash
behind her ears.

She drove her mother dotty.

When her mother said UP,

Kate was sure to say DOWN.

When her mother said SMILE,

you can bet Kate said FROWN.

When her mother said HIGH,
Kate just had to say LOW.

But her favorite words
were N-O spells NO!

No, no, no, no,
Katie mumbled and sighed.

NO, NO, NO, NO,
she grumbled and cried.

Her mom did her best
to get Kate to say YES…

offered ice cream…

and tap shoes…

a puppy, no less!

A dollhouse…

a pony…

a hat with a bow…

and still stubborn Katie
said N-O spells NO!

NO to a quarter

and NO to a kiss.

N-O to that
and N-O to this!

No, no, no, no,
Katie muttered and howled.

NO, NO, NO, NO,
she spluttered and yowled.

But Mom didn't holler,
and Mom didn't shout.

She thought

and she
thought

and she figured it out.

How did she do it?
I bet you can guess.

One day Mom said NO...

and so Katie said YES!